READING CHAMPION

The King with Horse's Ears

by Damian Harvey and Wazza Pink

Many years ago, there lived a king with tall, pointed ears. They looked just like a horse's ears.

When the king looked at them
in the mirror, they made him feel sad.
He was sure everyone would laugh if
they knew about his ears, so he kept
them a secret.

Every day, the king wrapped a long scarf around his head. Then he put his crown on top of it.

When he was not wearing his crown, the king wore a hat.

He had a special hat to wear in the bath ...

... and another one to wear in bed.

The king was good at keeping his secret.

He was so good that even the queen did not

know about his ears.

There was only one person that had ever discovered the king's secret. It had happened one day when the king needed a haircut. As the barber cut the king's royal hair, he saw the horse-ears. The king was very worried the barber would tell someone else his secret.

The king locked the barber in the tower room of the castle. "No one else must ever find out my secret," the king told him.

"You will stay here in the castle forever and only come down to cut my hair."

And so each month, the barber cut
the king's hair.

Many months passed. Then one day,
as he was cutting the king's hair,
the barber fell to his knees.

"Please let me go," he begged. "I must return home. My son is ill. I have to help look after my family."

Thinking of his own family, the king felt sorry for the barber.

"Promise me you will not tell anyone about what you have seen," he said.

The barber promised.

"Very well, then you are free to go," said the king.

The barber left the king's palace feeling very happy.

The barber knew he had been lucky to be set free. He was happy to be back with his family, but he could not stop thinking about the king's horse ears. Keeping the king's secret felt as hard as carrying a heavy stone around all the time. The barber wanted to tell the secret to someone, but he knew it would make the king angry.

The longer the barber kept the secret,
the worse he began to feel. Soon, keeping
the secret began to make him feel ill.
He could not work and could not sleep.

The doctor came to see him. The barber told her how bad he was feeling. He told her he was keeping a secret for the king.

"You need to tell someone the secret," the doctor told him. "If you do not, you may die."

"But if I tell anyone the secret," said the barber, "the king will have me killed." The doctor was wise and told the barber what he should do.

So, one dark night, the barber went into the middle of the forest. There stood a very old tree.

The barber laid his hands on its trunk and whispered his secret to the tree.

"The king has horse's ears! The king has horse's ears!"

As soon as the words left his lips, the barber began to feel better.

Time passed. Soon it would be the king's
birthday. He was planning a big party.
Many people were travelling to the palace
to celebrate.

One traveller passed through the forest on
his way to the palace. He spotted the tall tree.
"This wood will make a fine fiddle to play
for the king's birthday party," he said,
and he took out his axe.

On the day of the king's birthday,

the traveller stood in front of the king

and took out his fiddle. He began to play,

but instead of beautiful music, the fiddle

began to shout ... "The king has horse's ears!

The king has horse's ears!"

Everyone went quiet and stared at the king.

"Oh no!" thought the king. "I can no longer hide my ears. Everyone will hate me for the way I look." He sadly took off his crown and scarf and waited for the people to start laughing at him.

But instead of laughing, the people all cheered. "Hooray!" they shouted. "Our king is like no other king! He has horse's ears!"
The king was amazed and a smile slowly spread across this face.
He had never felt so happy in his life.

"Our king is the most special king in the world!" shouted the people. "Hooray!"

The people were right. Their king was different. Not only did he have ears like a horse, but he was also a kind and wise king. People travelled from miles around to meet him. He welcomed everyone, no matter who they were or what they looked like.

Story order

Look at these 5 pictures and captions.
Put the pictures in the right order
to retell the story.

1

The barber tells the tree his secret.

2

The kingdom love their special king!

3

The barber learns the king's secret.

4

The king lets the barber go.

5

The violin tells the king's secret!

Independent Reading

This series is designed to provide an opportunity for your child to read on their own. These notes are written for you to help your child choose a book and to read it independently.

In school, your child's teacher will often be using reading books which have been banded to support the process of learning to read. Use the book band colour your child is reading in school to help you make a good choice. *The King with Horse's Ears* is a good choice for children reading at White Band in their classroom to read independently.

The aim of independent reading is to read this book with ease, so that your child enjoys the story and relates it to their own experiences.

About the book

A kind king in a far off land hides his ears from everyone – even his wife, the queen! He has horse's ears on his head and he is afraid people will laugh if they find out. Then a magical violin changes it all.

Before reading

Help your child to learn how to make good choices by asking: "Why did you choose this book? Why do you think you will enjoy it?"

Ask your child about some of their favourite fairy tales or traditional tales. Then look at the cover with your child and ask: "Do you think the king likes his ears or not? Why?"

Remind your child that they can break words into groups of syllables or sound out letters to make a word if they get stuck.

Decide together whether your child will read the story independently or read it aloud to you.

During reading

Remind your child of what they know and what they can do independently. If reading aloud, support your child if they hesitate or ask for help by telling the word. If reading to themselves, remind your child that they can come and ask for your help if stuck.

After reading

Support comprehension by asking your child to tell you about the story. Use the story order puzzle to encourage your child to retell the story in the right sequence, in their own words. The correct sequence can be found on the next page.

Help your child think about the messages in the book that go beyond the story and ask: "What is more important: the way you look or the way you treat others? Why?"

Give your child a chance to respond to the story: "What was your favourite part of the story? Why?"

Extending learning

Help your child predict other possible outcomes of the story by asking: "What if the king had run away when the violin told his secret? Where would he be and how would he be feeling?"

In the classroom, your child's teacher may be teaching recognition of recurring literary features in stories and traditional tales. The story contains several examples you can look at together such as:

"very well, then", "many years ago", "one dark night", "from miles around". Find these examples in the story, think about how they help to structure the story and are often used to begin or end sentences.

Franklin Watts
First published in Great Britain in 2020
by The Watts Publishing Group

Series Editors: Jackie Hamley and Melanie Palmer and Grace Glendinning
Series Advisors: Dr Sue Bodman and Glen Franklin
Series Designers: Peter Scoulding and Cathryn Gilbert

A CIP catalogue record for this book is
available from the British Library.

ISBN 978 1 4451 7221 7 (hbk)
ISBN 978 1 4451 7222 4 (pbk)
ISBN 978 1 4451 7228 6 (library ebook)
ISBN 978 1 4451 7923 0 (ebook)

Printed in China

Franklin Watts
An imprint of
Hachette Children's Group
Part of The Watts Publishing Group
Carmelite House
50 Victoria Embankment
London EC4Y 0DZ

An Hachette UK Company
www.hachette.co.uk

www.reading-champion.co.uk

Answer to Story order: 3, 4, 1, 5, 2